'A [illegible]rming tale, with charming illustrations [illegible]ome acute observations.' *Junior*

'A gentle [illegible] a very positive message for young children.'
The Bookseller

'a delightf[illegible] . . . ideal for reading aloud with a lovely story [illegible] super appealing rabbit illustrations.'
Family Interest Magazine

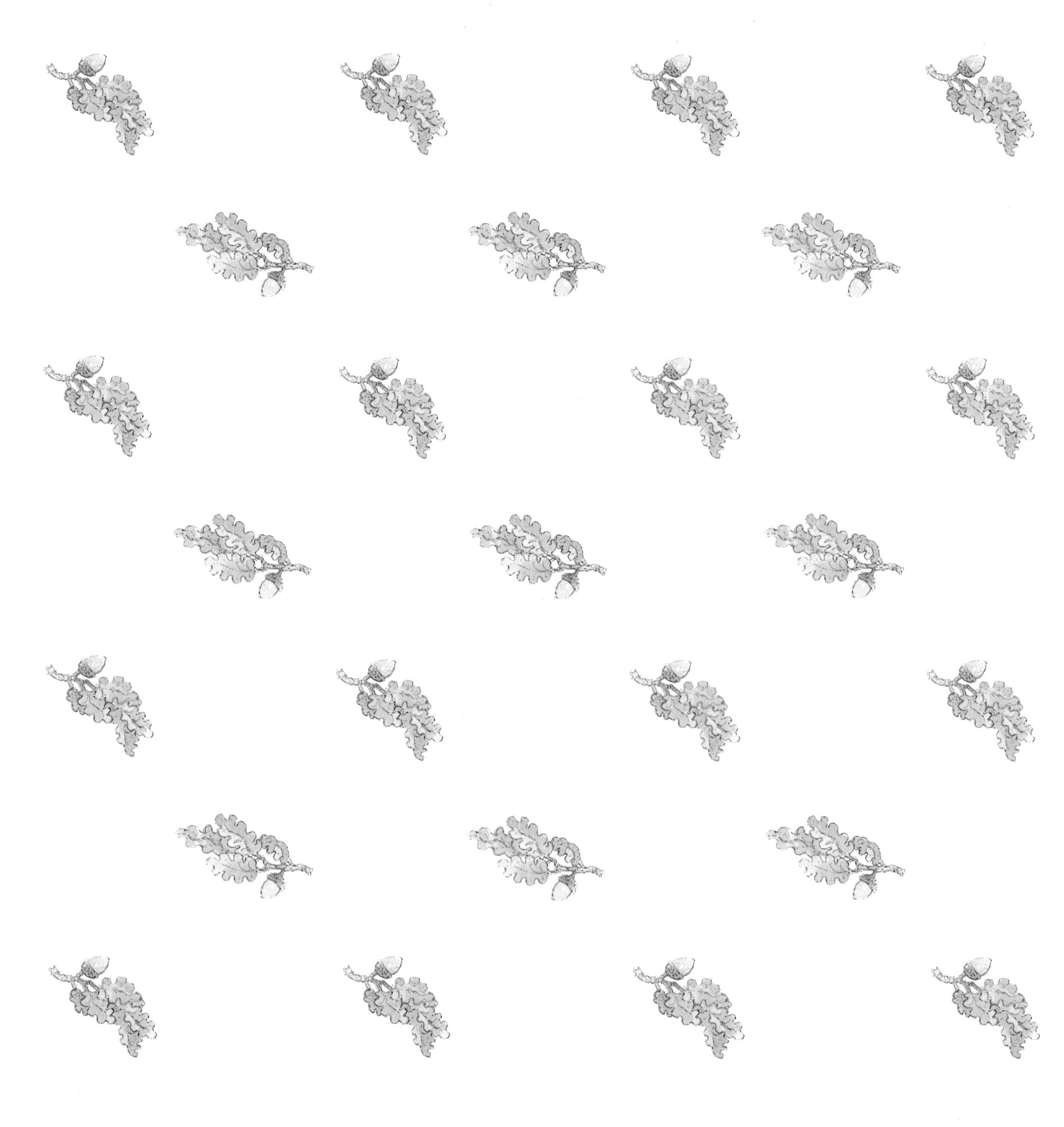

To Robin and Eunice *R L S*

For Jack and Edna *T K*

First published in Great Britain in 2004
by Orion Children's Books
This paperback edition first published in 2005
by Dolphin Paperbacks
a division of the Orion Publishing Group Ltd
Orion House
5 Upper St Martin's Lane
London WC2H 9EA

Design by Tracey Cunnell

A catalogue record for this book is available from the British Library.

Printed and bound in Italy

ISBN 1 84255 137 X

www.orionbooks.co.uk

Floppy Ears

Story by Ruth Louise Symes

Illustrations by Tony Kenyon

One day Twitchy Nose said, 'Can I go and play with my friends?'

'Can I go too?' said Floppy Ears.

'You're too little!' said Twitchy Nose.

'Take Floppy Ears with you or you don't go,' said Mum. 'And make sure the fox doesn't see you.'

'Oh all right, come on then, Floppy Ears,' said Twitchy Nose. 'You'll have to run fast to keep up with me.'

'Hello,' said Twitchy Nose's friends, Sneezer and Bendy Whiskers.

'Mum said I had to bring Floppy Ears with me,' said Twitchy Nose. 'What shall we play? I know, let's play hopping. I'm very good at hopping.'

‘Can I play?’ said Floppy Ears.
‘No – you’re too little to hop properly,’ said Twitchy Nose.

‘So what can I do?’ said Floppy Ears.
‘You can watch,’ said Twitchy Nose.

So Floppy Ears sat under the big old oak tree and watched Twitchy Nose and Sneezer and Bendy Whiskers hopping.

Floppy Ears thought Twitchy Nose was very good at hopping.

'Let's play racing now. I'm very good at racing,' said Twitchy Nose.

'Can I play?' said Floppy Ears.
'No – you're too little to race properly.'

'So what can I do?'
'You can watch.'

So Floppy Ears sat under the old oak tree and watched Twitchy Nose and Sneezer and Bendy Whiskers racing.

Floppy Ears thought Twitchy Nose was very good at racing.

'Let's play jumping over sticks now. I'm very good at jumping over sticks,' said Twitchy Nose.

'Can I play?' said Floppy Ears.
'No – you're too little to jump properly.'

'So what can I do?'
'You can watch.'

So Floppy Ears sat under the old oak tree and watched Twitchy Nose and Sneezer and Bendy Whiskers playing jumping over sticks.

Floppy Ears thought Twitchy Nose was very good at jumping.

'We have to go home now,' said Sneezer and Bendy Whiskers.
'That's OK,' said Twitchy Nose. 'I wanted to play by myself anyway. I'm going to play being a Mummy Rabbit.'

'Can I play?' said Floppy Ears.
'No – you're too little to play being a Mummy Rabbit.'

'So what can I do?' said Floppy Ears.

But Twitchy Nose was too busy playing to answer.
'I know what I can do,' Floppy Ears said. 'I can watch.'

While Floppy Ears was watching, the fox came over the hill.

'Twitchy Nose! Twitchy Nose!
The fox is coming!' cried Floppy Ears.

But it was too late.
The fox had seen them.

Floppy Ears and Twitchy Nose ran away as fast as they could.

'Quick! Let's hide in here,' said Floppy Ears.
Twitchy Nose and Floppy Ears jumped into a blackberry bush and kept very still.

The fox looked one way

and then it looked the other.

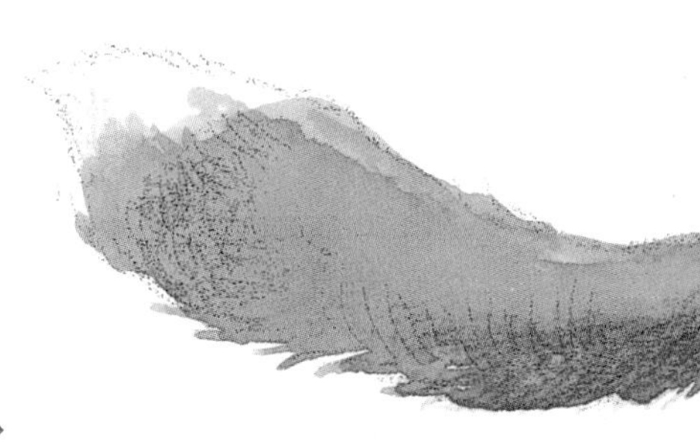

But it couldn't see Floppy Ears and Twitchy Nose.
They stayed quite, quite still until the fox had gone.

'Did you let Floppy Ears play?' Mum asked, when Twitchy Nose and Floppy Ears got safely home.

'Oh yes,' said Floppy Ears. 'We played hide and seek. We're very good at hiding.'

And Twitchy Nose said, 'Please can Floppy Ears come out to play again tomorrow?'

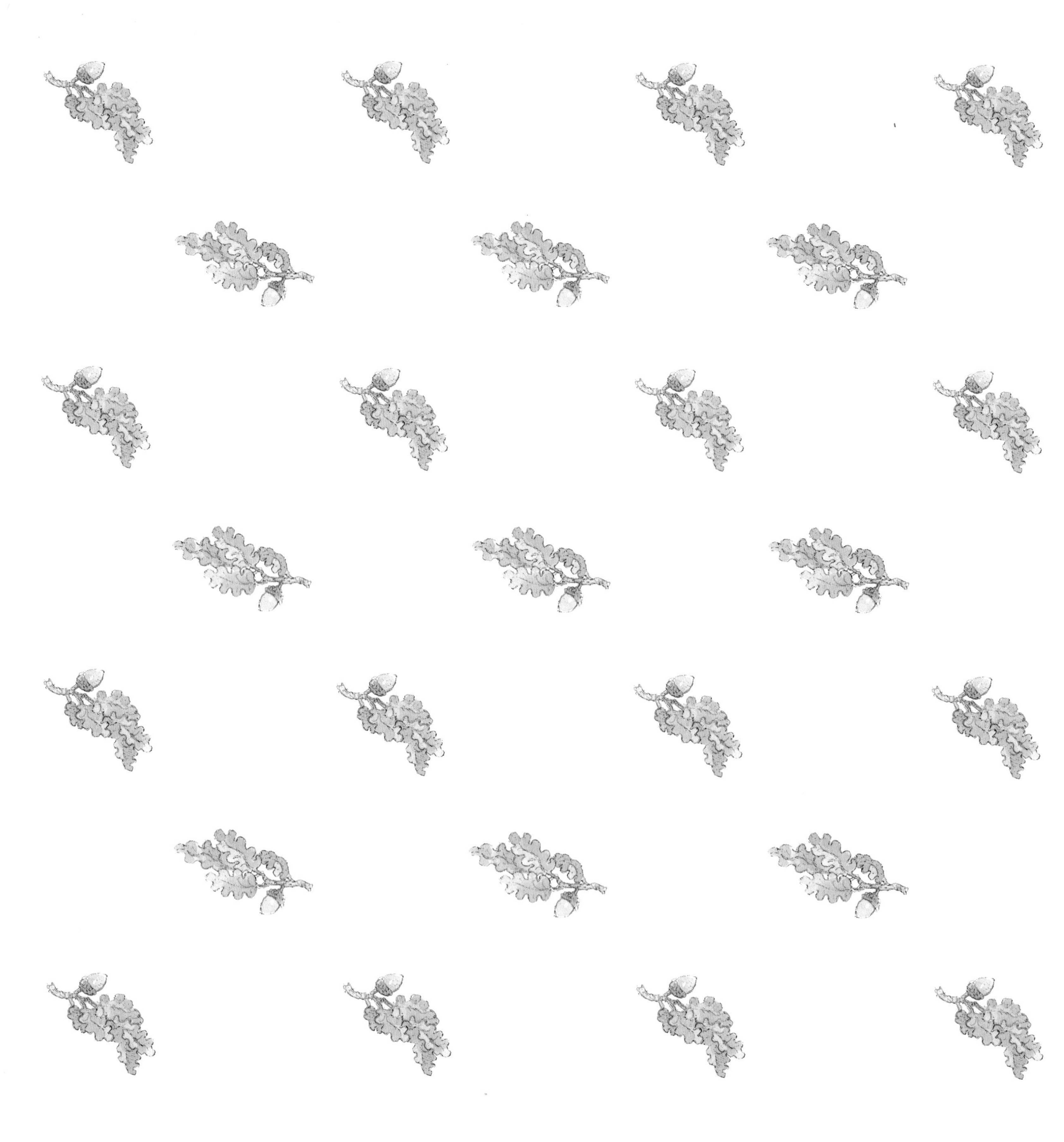